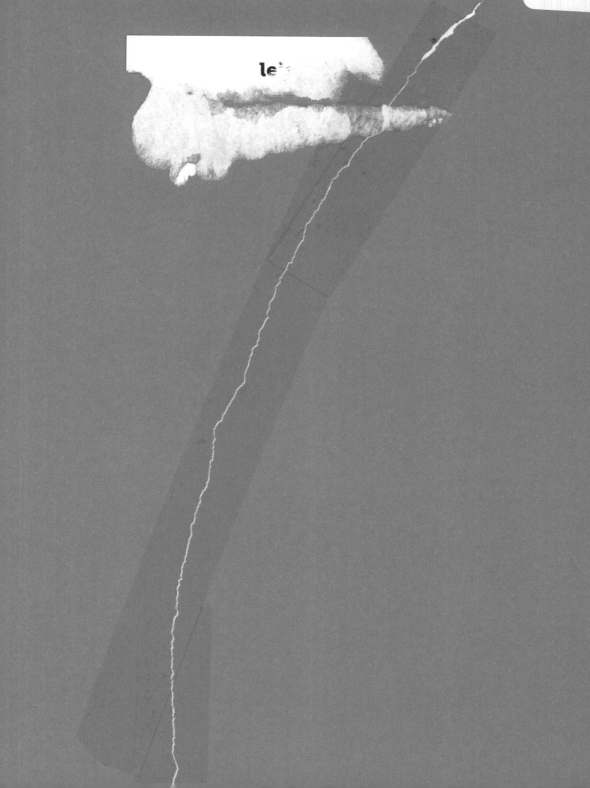

le

BRAVO, BORIS!

For my Mum and Dad x. – C.W.

For Toby 'Toto' Ridgway. – T.W.

OXFORD
UNIVERSITY PRESS

Great Clarendon Street, Oxford OX2 6DP

Oxford University Press is a department of the University of Oxford.
It furthers the University's objective of excellence in research, scholarship,
and education by publishing worldwide in

Oxford New York

Auckland Cape Town Dar es Salaam Hong Kong Karachi
Kuala Lumpur Madrid Melbourne Mexico City Nairobi
New Delhi Shanghai Taipei Toronto

With offices in
Argentina Austria Brazil Chile Czech Republic France Greece
Guatemala Hungary Italy Japan Poland Portugal Singapore
South Korea Switzerland Thailand Turkey Ukraine Vietnam

Text copyright © Carrie Weston 2011
Illustrations copyright © Tim Warnes 2011
The moral rights of the author and artist have been asserted

Database right Oxford University Press (maker)

First published 2011

British Library Cataloguing in Publication Data available

ISBN: 978-0-19-278978-5 (hardback)
ISBN: 978-0-19-278979-2 (paperback)

10 9 8 7 6 5 4 3 2 1

Printed in China

Paper used in the production of this book is a natural, recyclable product made
from wood grown in sustainable forests. The manufacturing process conforms
to the environmental regulations of the country of origin

Also available
Oh, Boris!
978-0-19-276338-9

Carrie Weston • Tim Warnes

BRAVO, BORIS!

OXFORD
UNIVERSITY PRESS

The day that Miss Cluck was
taking the class camping,
everyone was very excited.

When Miss Cluck said that it
was almost time to set off, all the
animals squealed with delight.

Leticia the rabbit
carried her butterfly net.

Maxwell the mole
clutched his Teddy.

The little mice
each had a basket.

Fergus the fox cub
was given the map.

Leticia

And Boris was put
in charge of . . .

absolutely everything else!
For Boris was an enormous,
hairy, scary, grizzly bear . . .
but he was also rather kind and helpful.

'Bravo!'
said Miss Cluck
as Boris heaved the
huge bag on his back.
'What would we
do without you?'

Scrap

Mini
Beasts

'Phew!'

Miss Cluck and her class set off through the woods.

'Whee!'

Leticia chased after butterflies.

Fergus puzzled over the map.

Maxwell got Teddy stuck up a tree.

And the mice struggled with their baskets.

Eventually Boris caught up with them all.

Poor Miss Cluck
blew her whistle.
'This really won't do,'
she said, 'we must
stay together.'

'But we're tired!'

Then Boris had an idea.

He found room for
everything in his bag.
Even the tired mice.

'Bravo, Boris!' cheered
his friends.

Before long they came to a little bridge.

Boris and Leticia dropped twigs into the stream.

'Come on, Boris!'

'Go, Leticia!'

Then everyone rushed to the other side of the bridge to see whose would come out first.

But somehow,
Boris forgot about the
bag on his back.

Somehow,
Maxwell's Teddy
went
splash!
into
the
water.

Somehow,
the mice managed
to cling on.

Maxwell let out an enormous wail.
'**Oh, Boris!**' he cried.

Poor Boris felt so clumsy and ashamed.

Miss Cluck carefully leaned over the bridge with Leticia's butterfly net, but it was no good. Teddy was floating away.

Boris decided it was time to be very brave. He leapt into the water . . .

splash!

all the way
up to his
hairy knees!

'Hurry,
Boris!'

Boris scooped Teddy safely out of the water.
Now there were two dripping-wet bears.

'Teddddy!'

And Maxwell
hugged
them both.

'Boris is the **biggest, bravest, best bear!'** said Maxwell.

'Bravo, Boris!'

'Bravo, Boris!' agreed Miss Cluck.
'Now let's set up camp before there are
any more accidents.'

The animals gathered around
while Miss Cluck explained
how to build a tepee.
It all sounded very easy.

Leticia and Maxwell collected long sticks.

The mice chewed off
some lengths of rope.

'Nibble!'   'Nibble!'

Boris helped
Fergus spread
out the canvas.

Then they all tried to put it together.

But it was not easy . . . not at all easy.

Once the tepee was up, the fun really began. Miss Cluck got out a new box of chalks and let everyone draw on the tepee.

Camp Cluck

It looked wonderful.
Boris put Maxwell's Teddy on top to dry . . .

and off they went to pick berries for supper. Miss Cluck showed them which ones were good to eat.

Boris carried the full baskets while the other animals hurried excitedly back to camp.

But they were in for a **shock!**

For their wonderful tepee wasn't
quite so wonderful any more.
Someone had drawn on Miss Cluck's face.
Someone had pulled down all the sticks . . .

Camp Cl

'No No
No!'

and someone was going to be
in **BIG** trouble!

Miss Cluck was very, very angry indeed.
She marched straight up to the bulging
canvas, reached underneath, and pulled out . . .

two very naughty little wolf cubs.
The cubs wriggled and struggled.

'Do your parents know you are out in the woods
alone?' asked Miss Cluck in her firmest voice.

'We don't care!' yelled one of the cubs rudely.
'Our daddy is a **big,**
bad
wolf!'

'Grrrrrr!'

'He's much **bigger** than you,' said the other,
even more rudely, 'and he **eats chickens** for . . .'

'Supper!' boomed Boris with a great big berry-stained grin.

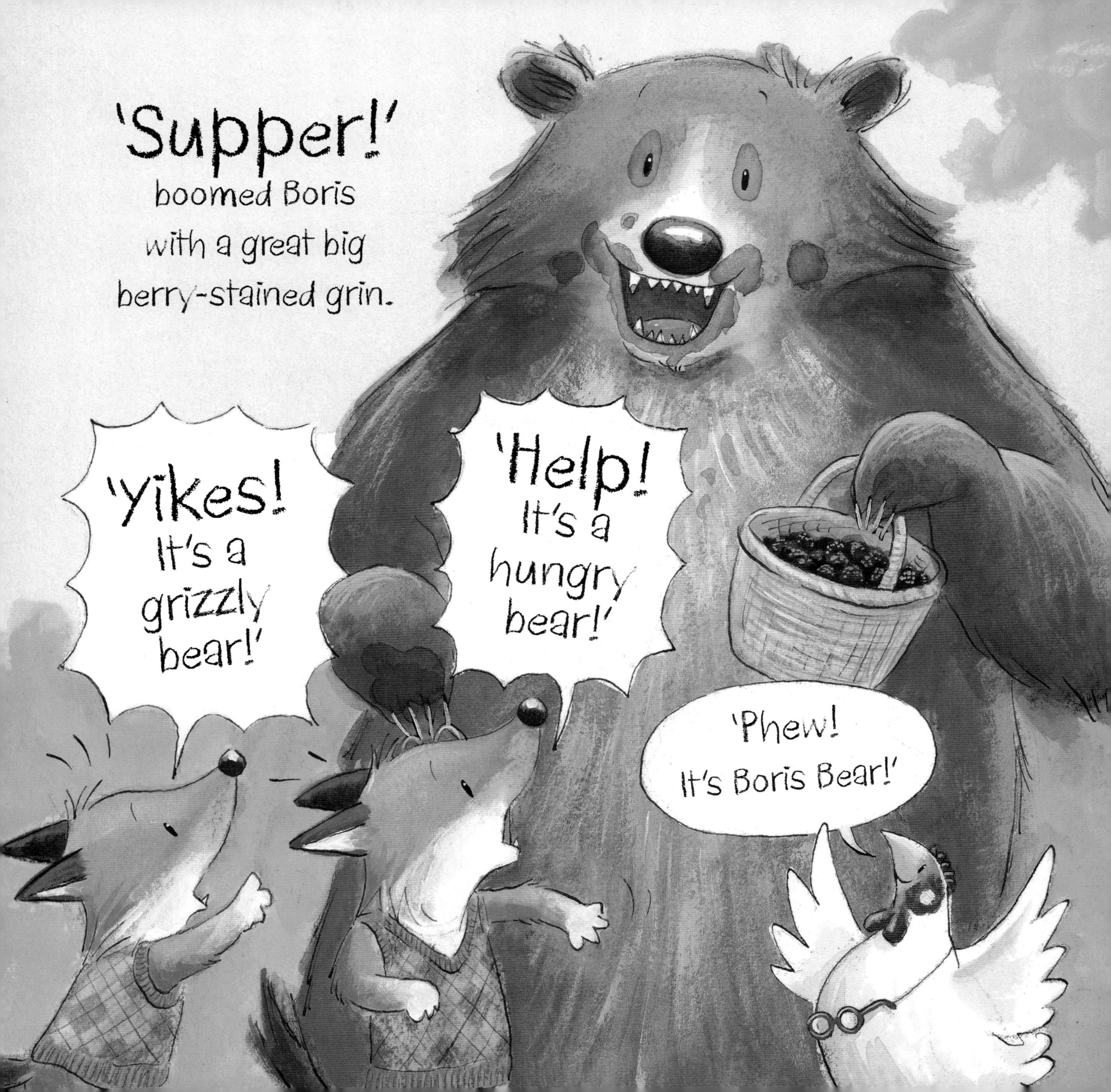

The naughty little wolf cubs
turned on their heels and fled.
Boris was most confused.

'Aaaaagghhh!'

'Oh, Boris, what a brave bear you are,'
smiled Miss Cluck,
'now let's
put the tepee
back together.'

'Bravo
for hairy,
scary Boris!'

That evening Boris and his friends ate a supper of toasted marshmallows and berries until the sun went down.

Then Miss Cluck got out her guitar and they sang songs under the stars.

'Kum Bay Ya!'

'Mmm yummy!'

Boris felt his eyelids grow heavy.
It was tiring being a big, brave bear.
'I think I might go to bed now,' he yawned.

'Sleep tight!'

'Good night, Boris.'

'Night night!'

Boris snuggled down happily inside the tepee and was soon snoring.

A little later, Fergus,
then Leticia, Maxwell
with Teddy, the mice,
and Miss Cluck crept
into the tepee.

There wasn't much room but nobody minded a bit.
After all, everyone had a nice, soft place to sleep . . .

even Miss Cluck.
'Bravo, Boris,' she whispered
as she fell asleep.